s, and at your new school, you have a new chance for more friendships!

Allais, Since this book is arriving late for your birthday, I would like for it to also be a gift marking your completion of preschool and beginning kindergarten in a new school. You have learned much, made great friendships, and you're ready for kindergarten now. I'm quite proud of you, Allais!

May 2017

For your age 5 birthday! I forgot to

Allais, this is a birthday gift I forgot to pack when I visited with you recently. So this is a little surprise for now. I love this book about good friends, and the wonderful pictures that help tell the story. I hope you like it too. I love you, Grandmama ♥

978-1-938700-39-2

Published by Commonwealth Editions, an imprint of Applewood Books, Inc.
P.O. Box 27, Carlisle, Massachusetts 01741

Visit us on the web at www.commonwealtheditions.com
Visit Shankman and O'Neill on the web at www.shankmanoneill.com

Printed in China

10 9 8 7 6 5 4 3 2 1

THE SEA LION'S FRIEND

BY
ED SHANKMAN

ILLUSTRATED BY
DAVE O'NEILL

Commonwealth Editions
Carlisle, Massachusetts

A sea lion passes his days in the waves.

And he lies on the rocks. And he sleeps in the caves.

And so, if he longs for a friend by the sea,

Well, then, these are the places the friend has to be!

But who else finds joy in the surf and the sun?

Who else thinks that lying on wet rocks is fun?

The real question is, after all, in the end:

Who wants to be a sea lion's friend?

And that's what the sea lion wondered one day.
He wondered when friendship would wander his way.
Could a friend just appear, right out of thin air?
If the sea lion blinked, would a new friend be there?

Did he think if he wished for a friend to come by,
That the friend who he wished for would fall from the sky?
Was it only pretend to believe in the end
That the wishes he wished could turn into a friend?

But then just as he wondered
If wishes come true,
As he questioned exactly
What wishes can do,

As he tried to believe
That a friend could appear,
A *seagull* flew down
And he landed right here!

Yes, he dropped
From the skies
Like a total surprise,
And was staring
The sea lion
Right in the eyes.

It was seagull and sea lion
There face to face,
Head to head, toe to toe,
In the very same place!

And though one was more fin and the other more feather,
They both knew somehow they'd be perfect together.

Sure, one had a snout and the other a beak,
And the one liked to bark while the other would squeak.
(Though I think some would say it was more of a shriek.)
But who cares what the sound is as long as you speak?

Who cares if one flew while the other was grounded,
Or if one was thin while the other was rounded?
Or if one was tall and the other was small?
Being *different*, you see, made no difference at all!

The ways they were different were easy to name,
But in time they would find they were much more the *same*!

They would laugh the same laughs.

They would dream the same dreams.

They would play the same games every day, and it seems
The things one liked to do, the other liked too —

They just seemed to see life from the same point of view.

And sometimes they tried a few things that were new!
(Though some worked out better than others, it's true.)

They explored the marina — the buoys and boats,
And they played on the docks and the posts and the floats.

Their togetherness had no beginnings or ends,
And they both knew how lucky they were to be friends.

In the mornings they'd stumble outside in their socks,
And build cities of rocks that they stacked just like blocks.

Then they locked all their rocks in a big blocky box,
With their socks and some clocks and a little stuffed fox.

Now and then, just for fun, they would run a few races.
Or slow down and quit after just a few paces.

And sometimes they hid in unusual places.
Of course, in some cases, they made funny faces.

In the late afternoons
They sang beautiful tunes,
Serenading the seals
While the loons played the spoons.

Then at night they'd retire
To sit by the fire,
And watch as the moon
Would rise higher and higher.

Sometimes they would spend half a day at the beach,
Learning all of the things that the other could teach.

And on days when the sea lion wanted to cook,
The gull entertained him with rhymes from this book!

THE SEA LION'S FRIEND

They were lounging around late one Friday in May,
When the sun set like fireworks over the bay.
And then once darkness fell, they reclined on a ridge,
Watching ships passing quietly under a bridge.

The steamships were grand
And the barges were flat.
They saw lightships and flagships —
What's cooler than that?
The tugboats were small
And the cruise ships were tall,
And their friendship, of course,
Was the best ship of all.

Yes, friendship, they found, was the best part of life,
For a boy and a dog or a husband and wife.
For a rose and a bee or a ghost and an elf,
They learned that what mattered was friendship itself!

And so, over time, as some friends like to do,
Our two friends befriended some other friends, too—
A cat and a flea, a goose and a gander,
A serious snake and a sweet salamander ...

… A shrimp and a fish and a fly and a snail,

And a duck on a dock and a whale with a pail.

He had wanted one friend when he didn't have any

And now that *one* friendship had led him to many!

It was friendship, you see, that made other things fun—
Like a dive through the waves or a flop in the sun,
And then long after all of the games were begun,
It was friendship that made it okay to be done.

Whatever they had, the two of them shared.

Whatever one broke, the other repaired.

One would be brave if the other was scared.
It was easy, you see, because both of them cared.

A friendship like that is a joy every day.

We depend on our friends.

We expect them to stay.

Which is why I am sure you'll agree when I say,

It can be very sad if a friend goes away.

But that is what happened one morning, you see,

When the sea lion woke up alone as can be.

He knew by the feeling,

He knew by the sound,

That his good friend the seagull was nowhere around.

He looked in the cave   And he looked on the rocks,

And he looked through the box with the socks and the fox.

And he looked to his left
And he looked to his right,
But it seemed that the seagull
Was nowhere in sight.

Where else could he be? Where on earth would he go?
Would the seagull come back? There was no way to know!
Why would a pal he had loved like a brother
Suddenly vanish to someplace or other?

But just as he heard himself questioning why,
As he wondered if friendship was passing him by,
He spied something small through the side of his eye—

A tiny
white
feather
that dropped
from
the sky.

Now, feathers don't fly by themselves, as you know.
There is something *above* when a feather's below.
So the sea lion stood and he looked to the air,
And I think you can guess who he saw way up there!

Yes, the seagull, that's who, and he'd brought something, too —
A big shiny box wrapped in purple and blue.
The sea lion pulled off all the ribbons and strings
And discovered they covered a cake fit for kings!

Yes, a big chocolate cake that was teeming with candles,
Perched on a platter with elegant handles.
It was sea lion's birthday! He almost forgot!
But lucky for him, the seagull had *not*.

And so, there they sat, sharing friendship and cake.
That's the best combination a baker can make.
Just two special friends in their favorite place,
Each with a big chocolate smile on his face.

So the sea lion's wish for a friend had come true.
He had found a new friendship right out of the blue.
(I wasn't so sure that would happen, were you?)
Well, it just goes to show you what *wishing* can do!

Now, some folks may think
Of this tale as pretend,

But our heroes defend
Every word that was penned.

And the seagull knows well
That while stories must end,

He will be, *forever,*
The sea lion's friend.

ALSO by Ed Shankman and Dave O'Neill

When a Lobster Buys a Bathrobe
My Grandma Lives in Florida
The Boston Balloonies
The Cods of Cape Cod
I Met a Moose in Maine One Day
Champ and Me by the Maple Tree
The Bourbon Street Band is Back

Also by Ed Shankman with Dave Frank

I Went to the Party in Kalamazoo

Ed Shankman

Ed Shankman's entire life has been one long creative project. He has been writing children's books since he himself was a child. He performed for many years as a lead guitar player and is an impassioned, if imperfect, painter. He is now planning to publish his novel, *The Backstage Man*, which was written over the course of three decades. And he has spent his professional career directing creative teams within the advertising industry. Today, Ed lives in New Jersey with his wife, Miriam, who is the love of his life, and their two cats.

Dave O'Neill

Dave O'Neill is an illustrator and art director. Throughout the years, Dave has worked with several advertising and marketing agencies as a graphic designer for children's brands. He also moonlights with an improv comedy troupe and designs toys in his spare time. More of Dave's work can be found on his art blog, at oneilldave.blogspot.com. Dave has a pet seagull named Sully. Or does he? (He doesn't.) Does he? Today, Dave is a husband to a cool girl and a father to a cool, smaller girl.

www.shankmanoneill.com